Set 1-A

HELLO! HELLO!

A LOOK INSIDE THE TELEPHONE

EVE & ALBERT STWERTKA
PICTURES BY MENA DOLOBOWSKY

JULIAN Ⓜ MESSNER

JULIAN MESSNER and colophon are
trademarks of Simon & Schuster, Inc.

Design by Malle N. Whitaker.
Manufactured in the United States
of America.

Lib. ed.
10 9 8 7 6 5 4 3 2 1
Paper ed.
10 9 8 7 6 5 4

**Library of Congress
Cataloging-in-Publication Data**
Stwertka, Eve.
    Hello! hello! : a look inside the
telephone / Eve & Albert
Stwertka : picures by Mena
Dolobowsky.
        p.   cm. — (At home with
science)
    Includes index.
    Summary: Provides a detailed
description of how a telephone
works.
    1. Telephone—Juvenile
literature.   [1. Telephone.]
I. Stwertka, Albert. II. Dolobowsky,
Mena.   III. Title.   IV. Series.
TK6165/S78 1991   91-12216
621.385—dc20   CIP   AC
ISBN 0-671-69459-6 (lib. bdg.)
ISBN 0-671-69465-0 (pbk.)

CONTENTS

REACH AROUND THE WORLD

Have you ever been caught in an emergency? If so, the telephone may have helped you out. With a telephone nearby, you could call for an ambulance, or a doctor, or the fire department, or the police.

The phone also helps people discuss business, chat with friends, or order tickets to a show. It keeps them in touch with others who are far away, even across the ocean.

Think of all the uses you have for the telephone. Make a list. It's going to be a long one.

The telephone can take the sound of your voice on an instant trip around the world. Even a giant in a fairytale could not roar loud enough to be heard that far away.

The name "telephone" comes from the Greek words *tele*, meaning distant, and *phone*, meaning voice.

Can you think of other words starting with *tele*? Write them down.

Before the telephone was invented, people could hear each other only as far as they could shout. To get in touch with someone out of shouting range, they had to send messages and letters. Messengers walked, ran, or rode on horseback all over the land. Sometimes they sailed across the sea. It could take them months to bring back the answer to a message.

Without a phone, how would you get in touch with someone far away? You could write a letter. Can you think of any other ways?

7

To call for help in emergencies, people in towns and villages found ways to make a loud noise. This way they could be heard for miles around. They rang church bells to signal a fire, flood, or war. Sometimes they shot off a cannon. In some parts of the world they beat drums.

They also sent signals by lighting huge bonfires. By day, the smoke could be seen from a long distance. At night, the glow was visible all around.

All these ways to communicate were slow, unreliable, and confusing. For instance, soldiers at war sometimes kept fighting long after the peace treaty was signed. Many were wounded or killed needlessly. But the battle continued until messengers arrived with the good news that the war was over.

Imagine living in a world without telephones. How would you keep in touch with friends? How would you get help in emergencies?

Today we are luckier. Good and bad news can be exchanged instantly by telephone. Armies can be kept informed. Leaders can talk to each other directly. Many misunderstandings can be avoided.

The phone also unites friends and families who live far apart. They can share a joke, get comfort and advice, or make a date to meet.

Are you thinking of giving a party? It's easy to invite your friends. All you have to do is call them on the telephone.

MAKING WAVES

If you drop a pebble into a pool of water, circles of waves begin to form at the spot where the pebble hit the water. The waves ripple out, one inside the other, in all directions. They are caused by the disturbance the pebble made in the water.

Sound is a wave, too. It is also caused by a disturbance. Like waves of water, sound waves spread and travel in all directions.

The ripples you *see* in the pool are vibrations of the water. The sounds you *hear* are vibrations of the air. Just say "Boo!" and you will start the air moving. The moving air makes waves. At the crest, or high point, of each wave, the air is under pressure and is very dense. The air is squeezed together, and there is a lot of it in one place. At the low point of the wave, the air is under less pressure and is thinner. Our ears can detect these rapid changes in the pressure of the air. That's what it means to hear a sound.

You can *feel* sound waves: Fold a piece of tissue paper or aluminum foil over a comb. Keep your lips apart and put them gently against the wrapped comb. Now hum a tune. The sound of your voice makes the paper or foil vibrate. Feel the vibrations on your lips. They are caused by the sound waves. Listen to the humming sound. How do you like the music you are making?

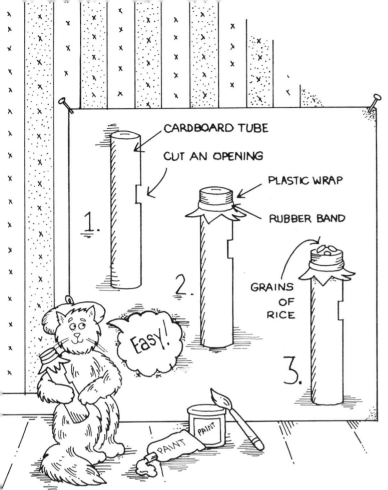

You can *see* the effect of sound waves:

This is best done with a helper. Take a cardboard tube of any length and carefully cut a hole in the side large enough for you to talk into. Stretch a piece of plastic wrap over one end of the tube and fasten it with a rubber band. Stand the tube upright. Place three or four grains of un-cooked rice on the covered end.

Now hold the tube steady. Ask your helper to hoot or sing into the opening you cut in the side. Watch the rice dance as the waves of air cause the plastic to vibrate.

13

Most sound waves are very complicated. When you speak or play the violin, you make wave patterns that go back and forth between high and low pressure. They change hundreds, even thousands, of times a second. It's amazing that our ears can interpret these patterns as speech and music.

Try making your own musical instruments. Here's a suggestion: Loop a rubber band around a door knob. Pull it out with one hand to form two strings. When you pluck the strings with your other hand, they twang like a banjo. Stretch the strings tight to make them vibrate fast and give off a higher-sounding noise. Relax them a bit to make them vibrate more slowly and give off a lower-sounding noise.

MAKING SOUND WAVES!

LET'S LOOK AT YOUR PHONE

Like ripples in water, sound waves in the air eventually die out as they travel outward. The wonderful thing about the telephone is that it can keep the sound waves made by your voice traveling on. It does this by changing your voice patterns into matching patterns of electricity.

When you talk into your phone, your words zip through the telephone wires in electrical form. They travel across the streets all the way to your friend's house. Here, your friend's phone changes the electric signals back into sound waves. And, presto, your friend is listening to the sounds of your voice.

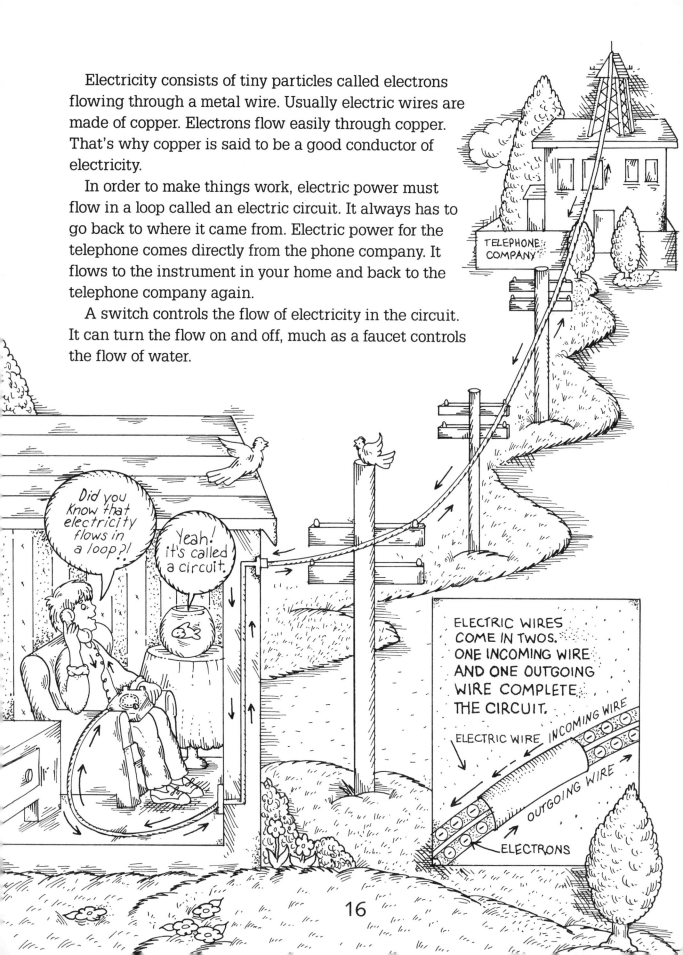

Electricity consists of tiny particles called electrons flowing through a metal wire. Usually electric wires are made of copper. Electrons flow easily through copper. That's why copper is said to be a good conductor of electricity.

In order to make things work, electric power must flow in a loop called an electric circuit. It always has to go back to where it came from. Electric power for the telephone comes directly from the phone company. It flows to the instrument in your home and back to the telephone company again.

A switch controls the flow of electricity in the circuit. It can turn the flow on and off, much as a faucet controls the flow of water.

16

The switch that opens and closes the telephone circuit is called a plunger. You can see it just below the handset on your phone. When the phone is not in use, the handset rests in the cradle and presses down the plunger. This interrupts the circuit, and no electricity flows.

When you lift the handset, the plunger springs up. The electricity starts to flow. If you put the receiver to your ear you'll hear the dial tone. It tells you that the telephone circuit is complete and ready for a call.

I keep getting a busy signal!

DIAL TONE!

INCOMING WIRE

OUTGOING WIRE

TELEPHONE COMPANY

INCOMING WIRE

OUTGOING WIRE

IN

OUT

PLUNGER

POP!

IN

OUT

PLUNGER

WHEN PLUNGERS ARE UP ELECTRIC SIGNALS CAN MOVE IN A COMPLETE CIRCUIT.

You can make your own electric circuit with two feet of appliance wire, a flashlight bulb, and a dry-cell battery. Strip the plastic off both ends of the wire. Tape one end to the bottom of the battery. Wrap the other end around the metal base of the bulb. Touch the base of the bulb to the top of the battery. The bulb lights because you've completed the circuit. Lift the bulb off the battery. The light goes out because the circuit is broken.

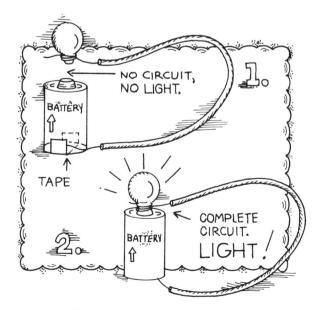

NO CIRCUIT, NO LIGHT.

1

BATTERY

TAPE

2

COMPLETE CIRCUIT.
LIGHT!

BATTERY

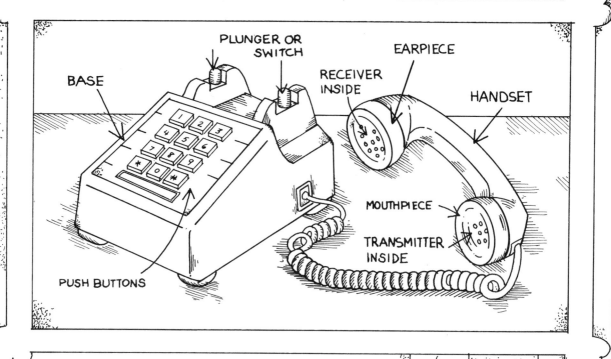

PLUNGER OR SWITCH

EARPIECE

RECEIVER INSIDE

HANDSET

BASE

MOUTHPIECE

TRANSMITTER INSIDE

PUSH BUTTONS

Look at the mouthpiece of your telephone handset. You will notice a protective cover with holes in it. Behind those holes is the device that changes the sounds of your voice into matching electrical patterns. This is called the transmitter.

The transmitter is made up of a shallow cup called a carbon chamber and a very thin piece of aluminum called a diaphragm. The edge of the diaphragm is held tight by the rim of the carbon chamber. But the center of the diaphragm is free to vibrate, like the skin of a drum.

The carbon chamber is filled with tiny grains of carbon. The carbon is similar to the charcoal you use for a barbecue. Carbon is not as good a conductor of electricity as copper. But it does let electrons flow through it. The closer the grains are to each other, the more easily the electricity will flow.

When you lift up the handset, the carbon chamber becomes part of the telephone circuit. Now electricity flows through the grains of carbon.

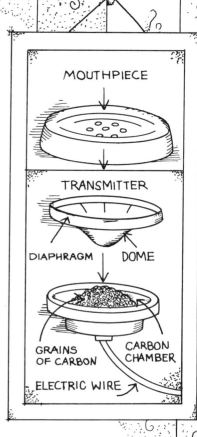

MOUTHPIECE

TRANSMITTER

DIAPHRAGM   DOME

GRAINS OF CARBON   CARBON CHAMBER

ELECTRIC WIRE

Fixed to the underside of the diaphragm is a small metal dome. It is pressed against the carbon in the carbon chamber. When you speak into the mouthpiece of the phone, the sound waves coming from your voice pass through the holes. They strike the diaphragm. The diaphragm and the dome vibrate in the exact same pattern as the sound waves.

Try this...

Tune your radio to the sound of someone speaking. Place a thin sheet of paper on top of the radio. Put 1/4 teaspoon of sugar on the paper. Notice how the vibrations of the voice cause the sugar crystals to dance around. In much the same way, your own voice activates the grains of carbon in your telephone.

The complicated vibrations of the dome affect the grains of carbon. During the high pressure part of the sound waves, the grains get pushed closer together. As a result, more electricity flows in the circuit. During the low pressure part, the dome puts less pressure on the carbon and the grains separate slightly. Because there is more space between them, less electricity flows in the circuit.

In this way, the transmitter makes an identical electrical copy of your voice patterns.

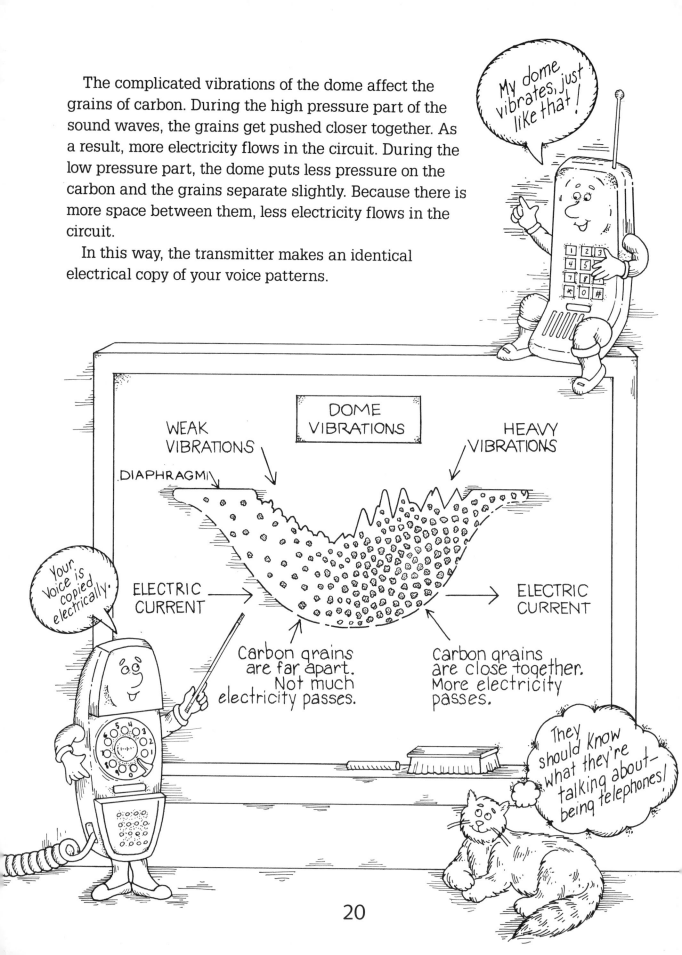

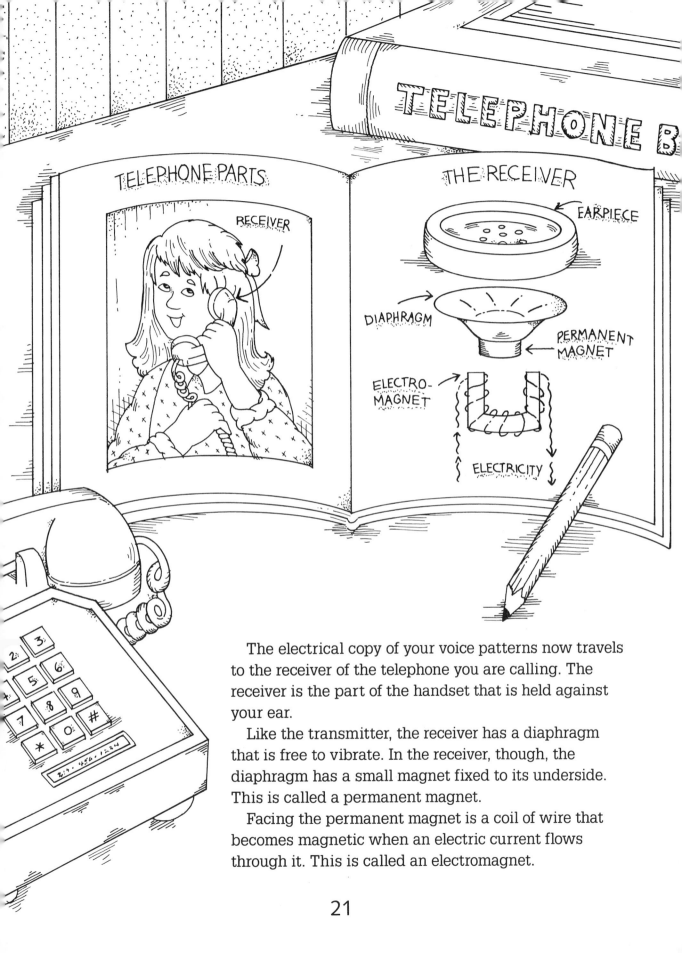

The electrical copy of your voice patterns now travels to the receiver of the telephone you are calling. The receiver is the part of the handset that is held against your ear.

Like the transmitter, the receiver has a diaphragm that is free to vibrate. In the receiver, though, the diaphragm has a small magnet fixed to its underside. This is called a permanent magnet.

Facing the permanent magnet is a coil of wire that becomes magnetic when an electric current flows through it. This is called an electromagnet.

21

The coil of wire carries the electrical copy of your voice patterns. The flow of electricity through this wire increases and decreases with the changing voice patterns. In turn, the electromagnet follows these changes. The stronger the electric current, the stronger the magnetism of the electromagnet.

Try this...

Wrap about two feet of appliance wire tightly around a large iron nail. Strip the plastic covering off both ends of the wire. Tape one end of the wire to the bottom of a dry-cell battery. Tape the other end to the top of the battery. This completes the circuit. The coil of wire has become an electromagnet. See how it attracts any small iron object you hold near it?

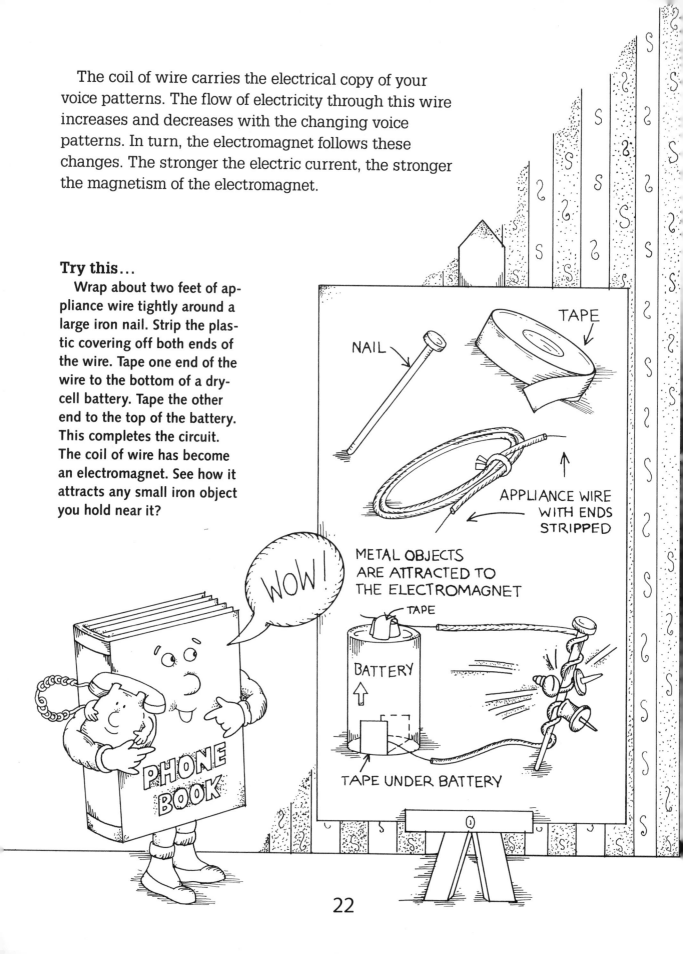

NAIL

TAPE

APPLIANCE WIRE WITH ENDS STRIPPED

WOW!

PHONE BOOK

METAL OBJECTS ARE ATTRACTED TO THE ELECTROMAGNET

TAPE

BATTERY

TAPE UNDER BATTERY

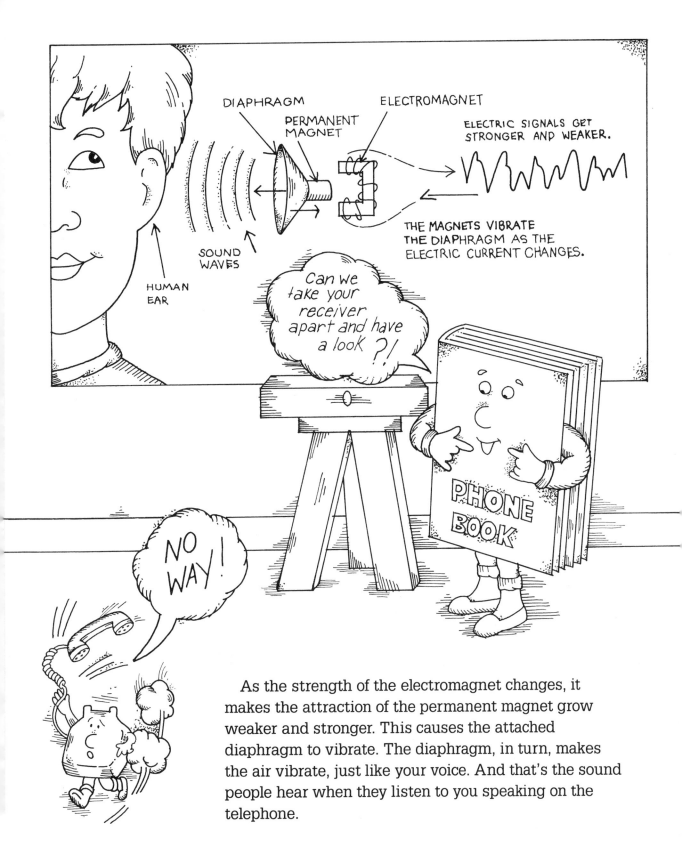

As the strength of the electromagnet changes, it makes the attraction of the permanent magnet grow weaker and stronger. This causes the attached diaphragm to vibrate. The diaphragm, in turn, makes the air vibrate, just like your voice. And that's the sound people hear when they listen to you speaking on the telephone.

23

NUMBER, PLEASE?

You need more than just a transmitter and a receiver to make a telephone call. There are more than 200 million telephones in the United States alone. How do you find your way to the telephone you want to reach?

This is the job of the central office of the telephone company. It completes the electric circuit between your telephone and the one you are calling.

You can make a single-wire telephone out of two empty tin cans and a ten-foot piece of string. You'll need a helper for this.

Using a hammer and nail, make a small hole in the center of the bottom of each can. Pass the ends of the string through the holes in the cans. Make a thick knot to keep the string from pulling out.

Take the cans to opposite sides of the room. The string must be *stretched tight*. Take turns talking into the can and putting it to your ear. Notice how much sound is transmitted.

In the early days of the telephone, customers were connected by a separate wire to every one of the other phones they might want to call. So many wires hung between buildings that they darkened the streets. In winter they often were covered with ice. Their weight could bring the poles crashing down.

Things improved when all the phone lines met in a central telephone building. Now, caller and receiver could be connected by a switchboard. But the earliest telephones didn't have numbers. Operators had to remember the name of every customer.

The first switchboard operators were young boys. They wore roller skates to speed them along on the job.

Every wire coming to the switchboard from an outside phone ended in a numbered opening called a "jack." A blinking light over the number meant that a call was coming in.

A boy would skate over, plug a wire into the jack of the caller and ask: "Number please?" Then he plugged a connecting wire into the jack of the number desired. This completed the circuit and the two people could talk.

To tell the second customer that a call was coming, the operator cranked a handle to ring a bell.

Zooming along on roller skates, the boys had many spills and crashes. Sometimes they also played pranks on the customers. Before long, they were replaced by adult operators who were more formal and polite.

Today, almost all calls are made by dialing the number directly. This system uses thousands of off-and-on switches called relays. The relays act like doors that lead you, one by one, to the telephone you want to reach. The number you dial tells the relays which doors to open.

Suppose you want to call a friend whose telephone number is 555-1234. The first three numbers, 555, identify the central telephone office of the phone you are trying to reach. The last four numbers select the particular telephone you want.

If you are making a long distance call, you need an additional set of numbers called an area code. For instance, the area code 312 selects Chicago as the city you are calling.

Let's say you dial the number 5 on a rotary dial. The electric circuit to the central office is interrupted five times while the dial returns to its rest position. On a Touch-Tone phone, you hear a musical note when you press the button labeled 5. This note sends the same information to the central office as the five clicking sounds you hear when you use a rotary dial. This information is instantly translated into switching signals in the central office.

29

One by one the numbers you dial tell the relays which doors to open. At the last number, a signal starts your friend's phone ringing.

Your friend lifts the handset to answer. This releases the plunger and closes the circuit. The last link between your two phones is complete. "Hi," you say. "It's me."

GIANT LEAPS

Until quite recently, phones were mainly linked together by wires. You can still see telephone wires strung on poles along the streets. In big cities they are often buried underground, and out of sight.

To carry calls from one continent to another, wires are bundled together in thick cables and strung along the ocean floor. These cables are thousands of miles long.

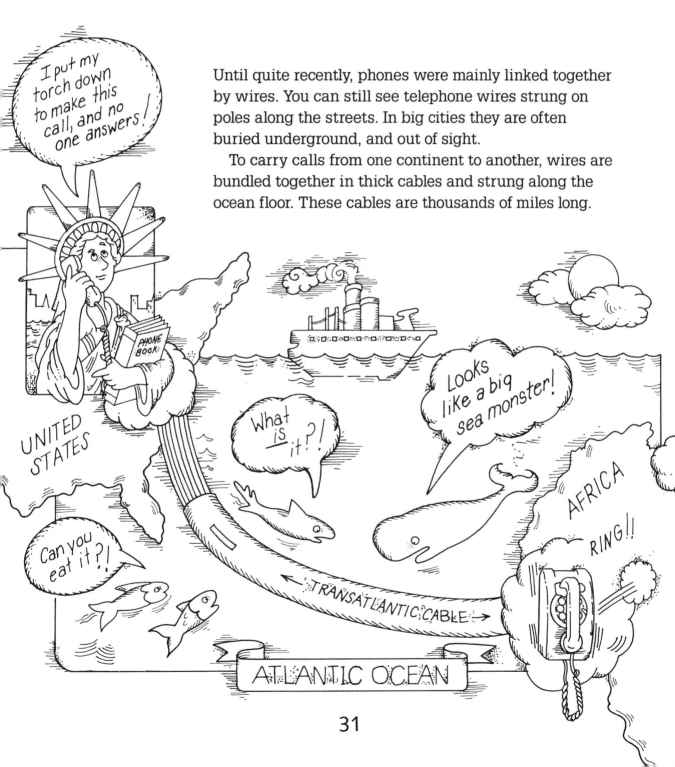

Today the telephone no longer has to depend on wires strung across mountains or under large bodies of water. Because sound waves can now be changed into radio signals, part of the wire circuit can be replaced by radio.

Most radio signals don't travel very far, though. To make them reach farther, a system of relay stations is needed.

Notice what happens to your favorite radio station when you are traveling in a car. When you are about thirty or forty miles away from home, the signal begins to fade until you can't hear it anymore.

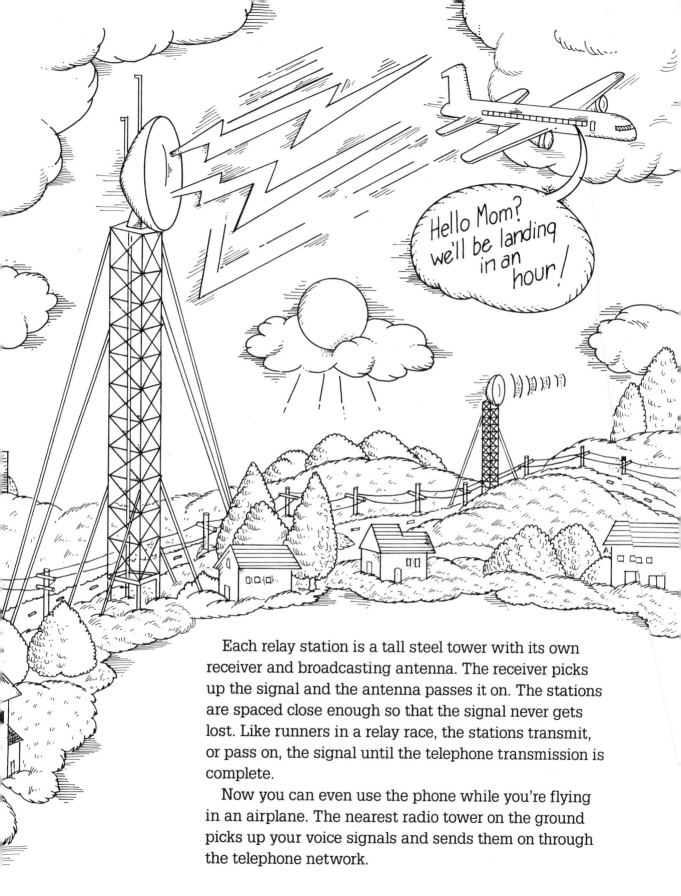

Each relay station is a tall steel tower with its own receiver and broadcasting antenna. The receiver picks up the signal and the antenna passes it on. The stations are spaced close enough so that the signal never gets lost. Like runners in a relay race, the stations transmit, or pass on, the signal until the telephone transmission is complete.

Now you can even use the phone while you're flying in an airplane. The nearest radio tower on the ground picks up your voice signals and sends them on through the telephone network.

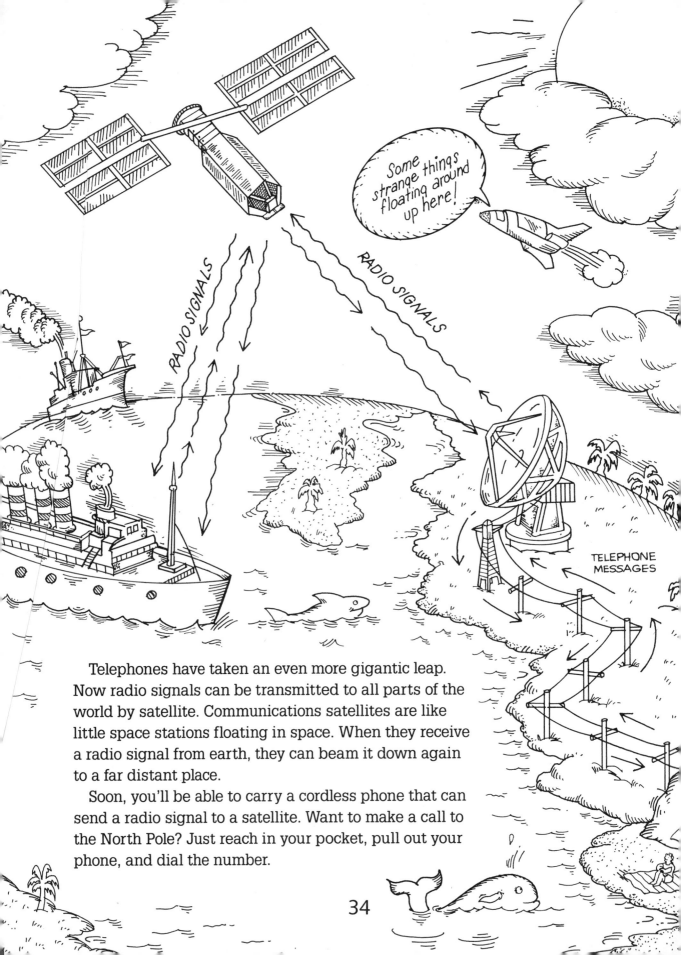

Telephones have taken an even more gigantic leap. Now radio signals can be transmitted to all parts of the world by satellite. Communications satellites are like little space stations floating in space. When they receive a radio signal from earth, they can beam it down again to a far distant place.

Soon, you'll be able to carry a cordless phone that can send a radio signal to a satellite. Want to make a call to the North Pole? Just reach in your pocket, pull out your phone, and dial the number.

CORDLESS PHONE

Cordless phones are already being used around the home. They look very much like ordinary phones, but no wire connects the handset with the base. The base is actually a radio that sends signals to the handset.

With a cordless phone you are free to move from room to room. You can even call from your garden. But that's about as far as you can go. The signal sent by the transmitter is too weak to travel much farther than 1,000 feet.

If you want to make phone calls while you are riding in a car, you have to use a cellular phone. This name comes from the way phone companies divide a city or countryside into smaller areas, called cells. Each cell is only a few miles across. It has its own receiver and radio transmitter. .

As you ride along, you pass through cell after cell. Computers automatically transfer your call from one transmitter to the next. The sound is as clear as if you were speaking from your living room.

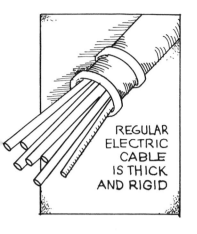

REGULAR ELECTRIC CABLE IS THICK AND RIGID

Recently, scientists have also discovered that they can send messages by changing sound signals into light signals. These signals are carried by *fiber-optic cables* made up of hundreds of glass fibers, each as thin as a hair. Each fiber can carry thousands of messages.

As you can see, the telephone combines easily with other kinds of technology. Computers built into your home phone, for example, can take messages and remember numbers. Telephones are certainly getting smarter and smarter.

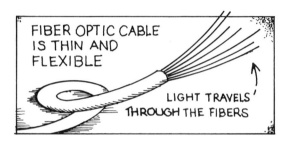

FIBER OPTIC CABLE IS THIN AND FLEXIBLE

LIGHT TRAVELS THROUGH THE FIBERS

Soon, the telephone may show you a picture of the person you are talking to. What are some other things you'd like your telephone to be able to do? Write them down. You'll probably have some interesting ideas.

GLOSSARY

Cables (KAY-bulls) Telephone wires fastened together in bundles.

Carbon chamber A shallow cup in the telephone transmitter that contains grains of carbon or charcoal. It is part of the phone circuit.

Cellular phone (SELL-you-lur FON) A phone that can be used in traveling vehicles. As it moves, it receives and transmits signals from different areas, or "cells."

Communications satellite (ku-mew-nuh-KAY-shuns SAT-uh-lite) A small space station that receives radio signals from earth and sends them down again to a distant place.

Conductor (kun-DUCK-ter) A material that lets electricity flow through it easily.

Cordless phone A phone in which the base and the handset are connected by radio transmission instead of by a wire.

Dial tone The sound we hear on the phone, telling us that it is ready to be used.

Diaphragm (DY-uh-fram) A thin piece of aluminum in telephone transmitters and receivers. Its vibrations transmit voice signals.

Electric circuit (uh-LEK-trik SIR-kit) The loop that electricity flows through from the power source and back again.

Electricity (uh-lek-TRIS-i-tee) The flow of electrons through a wire.

Electromagnet A coil of wire that becomes magnetic when electricity flows through it.

Electrons (ee-LEHK-trahns) Tiny particles that are part of the building blocks of all matter.

Fiber-optic cable (FY-bur AHP-tik KAY-bull) A cable that uses light instead of electricity to carry telephone signals.

Handset The part of most phones that is held in the hand, for speaking and listening.

Jacks The openings in a switchboard for the incoming and outgoing telephone wires.

Magnet Usually a form of iron or steel that can attract other things made of iron or steel.

Plunger (PLUN-jur) The switch on the phone that opens and closes the telephone circuit.

Receiver (ree-SEE-vur) The part of the phone you hold to your ear. It changes electric patterns into the sounds of speech.

Relay (REE-lay) One of the many off-and-on switches used in direct dialing that lead your call to the desired number.

Relay station A radio station that receives radio signals from the telephone and broadcasts them farther. It is part of a system for long distance calls.

Rotary dial (RO-tu-ree DILE) A phone dial that has to be turned to send switching signals to the central office.

Sound waves The movement of the air when it is disturbed by sound. Sound waves travel and spread in all directions.

Switchboard A central device for connecting the phone lines of many different callers and receivers.

Telephone An instrument for making the voice reach across a distance. From the Greek words *tele*, distant, and *phone*, voice.

Touch-tone A phone dial that has buttons to push for sending switching signals to the central office.

Transmitter The part of the phone you speak into. It changes the sounds of your voice into matching electric patterns.

Vibration (vy-BRAY-shun) A back-and-forth movement, like shaking or trembling.

INDEX